For Gemk,

Whose endless supply of ideas and honest critique made this possible.

感謝 Gemk

源源不絕的靈感及誠懇的建議讓這一切成真。

The **Little** White Lie

愈滾愈大的小謊話

Coleen Reddy 著

王 平 繪

薛慧儀 譯

Leo was watching cartoons on television.
He was eating lollipops at the same time.
He was having so much fun that he didn't notice that
he had eaten a whole bag of lollipops.

里歐正在看電視上的卡通，
一面還吃著棒棒糖。
他實在是太開心了，竟然不知不覺就吃掉了整包棒棒糖。

3

His mom, Mrs. Naggy, came home.

"Leo!" she screamed. "How could you eat a whole bag of lollipops?"

"I...I...." stammered Leo. He couldn't get out of it.

He was caught red-handed.

His mother said that if he ever did something like that,

he would be grounded for two weeks!

他的媽媽，南姬太太回家了。

「里歐！你怎麼可以把整包棒棒糖都吃掉了呢？」她大叫。

「我⋯我⋯」里歐支支吾吾地說不出話來。

他當場被捉個正著，想賴也賴不掉。

他的媽媽曾經說過要是他這樣做，就要被禁足兩個星期！

The only thing he could do was lie. Just a little white lie.
Everyone told little white lies.

"It wasn't me. It was...Nick," said Leo. Nick was his best friend.

"Nick came over earlier and ate them," Leo continued to lie.

"What a terrible thing to do! It's unhealthy to eat so much candy.
I'm going to phone his mom right now and tell her," said Mrs. Naggy.

"No," said Leo. "It's not his fault. He has some illness. He has to eat
lots of candy and sweets or he'll die."

Mrs. Naggy shook her head and walked away.

於是他只好說謊，只是一個小小的謊話啦！
反正每個人都會說點小謊的呀！
「不是我吃掉的，是…是尼克吃的啦！」里歐說。尼克是他最好的朋友。
「尼克剛剛來家裡，他把所有的棒棒糖都吃掉了。」里歐繼續撒著謊。
「真荒唐！吃這麼多糖果對健康一點好處也沒有！
我現在就去打電話告訴他媽媽。」南姬太太說。
「不要！」里歐說。「那不是他的錯，他生病了，
需要吃很多糖果和甜點，不然就會死掉耶！」
南姬太太搖了搖頭後，就走開了。

Leo thought that he had told a white lie and gotten away
with it, but it was not so.
A few days later, Nick had dinner at his house.
Just as he was helping himself to some tasty lamb,
Mrs. Naggy stopped him.

里歐以為他只是說了個小謊，應該不會有事了，但其實不然。
幾天後，尼克到里歐家裡吃晚餐。
就在尼克想要吃點鮮美的羊肉時，南姬太太阻止了他。

"Leo told me about your illness. I prepared this just for you."
She gave him a plate of food that was sweetened.
YUCK! Sweet rice and sweet lamb and sweet vegetables.
"What are you...?" Nick was about to ask what was going on
when Leo kicked him under the table.

「里歐告訴我你生病的事了，所以我特別為你準備了這個。」

她遞給尼克一整盤甜的食物。

喔！好噁心哪！甜的飯、甜的羊肉，還有甜的蔬菜呢！

「這是⋯？」尼克正想開口問這是怎麼回事時，里歐趕緊在桌下踢了踢他。

Later, Leo explained everything to Nick.

"Well," said Nick. "It's a lie for a lie. I lied for you, now you must lie for me."

"What are you talking about?" asked Leo.

"I want you to lie to my mother and tell her that she has to buy that new computer game for me. Tell her we need it for computer class and your mother bought one for you."

過了一會兒，里歐把一切都解釋給尼克聽。

「好吧！那我們就來個謊言交換吧！我替你說謊，現在你也要幫我說謊。」尼克說。

「你在說什麼呀？」里歐問。

「我要你對我媽媽撒謊，告訴她得買那套新的電腦遊戲給我，就說我們上電腦課的時候要用，而且你媽媽已經幫你買了。」

"That's stupid," whispered Leo. "Who would believe a stupid thing like that?"
"My mother will believe it," said Nick.
Leo had no choice. His "little white lie" was turning into big ugly lies.

「這太蠢了吧?! 誰會相信這麼遜的謊話?」里歐小聲地說。
「我媽媽就會相信。」尼克說。
里歐沒有選擇,他「善意的小謊言」已經變成不太妙的大謊言了。

15

Leo went to Nick's house and spoke to Mrs. Alot.
"My mom bought me this cool new game. We have to buy it for computer class. Are you going to buy one for Nick, too?"
"If your mom thought it was okay to buy it for you, then I'll get one for Nick. But I'm very surprised about this. I'm going to call your computer teacher, Mr. Mondo, and ask him what's going on."

里歐來到尼克家裡，對尼克的媽媽雅洛特太太說：
「我媽媽買了一個很酷的電腦遊戲給我，每個人都要買，
因為上電腦課要用到。妳也會買一套給尼克嗎？」
「如果你媽媽覺得可以買給你，那我也會買一套給尼克。
不過我對這件事感到很訝異，我等一下會打電話給
你們的電腦老師蒙多先生，問問他是怎麼回事。」

17

"No!" cried Nick and Leo.

"Mr. Mondo is very sick. He is in the hospital," said Leo.

"I'll send him a 'get well' card then," Mrs. Alot said.

"No!" cried Leo again. "He broke his leg."

"But he can read," Mrs. Alot replied.

"No, he hurt his eyes and he's blind now," said Leo.

「不行！」尼克和里歐同時叫了出來。

「蒙多先生病得很重呢！他現在在醫院裡。」里歐說。

「那我得送他一張祝他早日康復的卡片。」雅洛特太太說。

「不行！」里歐又叫了出來。「他摔斷腿了。」

「但他還是可以看卡片呀！」雅洛特太太回答說。

「不行！他傷到眼睛，所以現在瞎了。」里歐說。

"WOW!" cried Nick. "You're so good at lying. You have a gift."
Leo wasn't happy. He was worried about all the lying he had
done. He was afraid that someday he would slip up and then
his mother would know everything.

But he soon forgot his worries when Nick's mom bought the
new computer game. They played all day.

尼克還稱讚他：「哇喔！你真會說謊，你真是天生的說謊專家！」
但里歐卻不快樂，他很擔心自己撒的謊話，深怕哪天會不小心說溜嘴，
那媽媽就什麼都知道了。
不過他很快就把煩惱忘得一乾二淨，因為尼克的媽媽買了新的電腦遊戲，
他們倆玩了一整天。

21

The next day, Leo went with his mom to the supermarket.
He almost dropped dead when they ran into Nick and his mom.
"Hello, Mrs. Alot," said Leo's mom. "Say, why didn't you tell
me about the illness that Nick has? I didn't know that he had
to eat so much sugar."

第二天，里歐和媽媽一起去超級市場。
當他們碰見尼克和他媽媽的時候，里歐差點沒當場昏倒。
「你好，雅洛特太太！對了，你怎麼沒告訴我尼克有這種怪病呀？
我不知道他要吃這麼多糖呢！」里歐的媽媽說。

"What are you talking about?" asked Mrs. Alot. "Anyway, I wanted to talk to you about Mr. Mondo, the computer class teacher. Did you know that he broke his leg and he's blind as well?" Just then, when Leo thought things couldn't get any worse, he saw Mr. Mondo.

「你在說什麼呀？」雅洛特太太說。「不過，我早就想和你談談蒙多先生的事了，就是那個電腦老師呀！你知道他摔斷了腿，眼睛也瞎了嗎？」就在里歐覺得情況已經糟到不能再糟的時候，他看到了蒙多先生。

"Did someone say my name?" asked Mr. Mondo.
"Oh! I'm glad to see that you're better," said Mrs. Alot, looking very surprised. "I wanted to talk to you. Why are you asking the students to buy computer games for your class?"

「有人提到我的名字嗎?」蒙多先生問。

「喔!我真高興您看起來好多了。」雅洛特太太說,臉上表情看起來非常驚訝。「我早就想和您談談,為什麼要學生買電腦遊戲在電腦課用呢?」

"What are you talking about?" asked Mr. Mondo. "I never asked any of my students to buy computer games and I haven't been sick either."

Everyone was quiet. Then they realized that Leo and Nick had disappeared.

「您在說什麼呀？」蒙多先生問。「我從來沒有要學生買電腦遊戲呀！
而且我也沒有生病啊！」
一時之間，大家都鴉雀無聲，然後他們發現里歐和尼克不見了。

If you visit the neighborhood where Leo and Nick live, you're sure to see them. Until their mothers and Mr. Mondo think they've learnt their lesson, they will be mowing their neighbors' lawns. They don't get paid for it. There is a big sign at the supermarket that reads:

"Two *healthy boys looking for lawns to mow.*
Will not charge any money. FREE!
Serving time for telling lies!"

Do you need your lawn mowed?

如果你來到里歐和尼克家附近，你一定可以見到他們。
直到他們的媽媽和蒙多先生覺得他們得到足夠的教訓前，
他們得一直幫鄰居割草，而且還沒有薪水可拿！
在超級市場那裡，有個大大的牌子這樣寫著：
　　　　「兩個健康強壯的男孩應徵割草工作。
　　　　　不需任何費用，完全免費！
　　　　　這是他們說謊的懲罰。」
你家的草坪需不需要請人來整理一下呢？

聽寫拼字遊戲
Crosswords

小朋友，讓我們跟著里歐一起來玩這個遊戲，玩之前先按下 track 3，跟著里歐把單字念兩遍，然後按下 track 4 之後，你會聽到中文題目的部分，但括弧裡的中文會用英文念出來，這個時候呢，你就要把英文拼出來，跟著題號填在表中。

sugar game lawn lollipop

rice healthy mow leg

hospital lie cartoon

	(7)		1				
	(1)			2			
			(2)				
					3(3)		
(4)							
(5)		4					
(6)							

直的 (Down)

1. 被騙買了電腦（遊戲）給。

2. 吃了一整包的（棒棒糖），被媽媽臭罵了一頓。

3. 和說謊的懲罰是割鄰居的（草地）。

4. 煮了甜的（飯）給吃。

橫的 (Across)

(1) 超級市場的牌子上寫說和是（健康的）男孩。

(2) 和說謊的懲罰是（割）草坪。

(3) 說的（腿）斷了。

(4) 撒謊說因為受傷而被送去（醫院）。

(5) 在看（卡通）的時候，吃了很多棒棒糖。

(6) 說是（說謊）的專家。

(7) 騙說需要吃很多的（糖）。

生字表

 p. 2

lollipop [`lalɪ,pap] 名 棒棒糖

 p. 4

scream [skrim] 動 尖叫，大叫

stammer [`stæmɚ] 動 結結巴巴地
　　說

red-handed [`rɛd`hændɪd] 形 當場
　　被逮到的

ground [graʊnd] 動 禁足

 p. 6

illness [`ɪlnɪs] 名 疾病

 p. 8

get away with 成功逃避…

 p. 10

sweeten [`switn̩] 動 使變甜

 p. 14

whisper [`hwɪspɚ] 動 小聲說話

 p. 20

gift [gɪft] 名 天分

slip up 說溜嘴

 p. 22

run into 遇到…

 p. 30

mow [mo] 動 割草

lawn [lɔn] 名 草坪

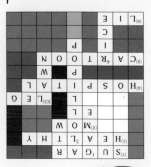

全新創作 英文讀本

帶給你優格（yogurt）般，青春的酸甜滋味！

Teens' Chronicles

愛閱雙語叢書

青春記事簿

大維的驚奇派對／秀寶貝，說故事／杰生的大秘密
傑克的戀愛初體驗／誰是他爸爸？
叛逆大維打工記／外星老師來上課／耶！放假了！

附中英雙語CD
（共八冊）
適讀年齡：10歲以上

你我身上純真的影子，
透過一篇篇幽默風趣的故事重現，
推薦你這套青春無悔的創作系列，
讓愛玫、杰生、大維、凱爾、海倫、傑克，
帶你進入他們的世界，品味另一種學習英語的全新感受。

國家圖書館出版品預行編目資料

The Little White Lie:愈滾愈大的小謊話 / Coleen
Reddy著; 王平繪; 薛慧儀譯.－－初版一刷.－－
臺北市; 三民, 2003
　　面; 公分－－(愛閱雙語叢書.二十六個妙朋
友系列) 中英對照
ISBN 957-14-3767-0　(精裝)

1. 英國語言－讀本

523.38　　　　　　　　　　　　　92008808

© The Little White Lie
—— 愈滾愈大的小謊話

著作人　Coleen Reddy
繪　圖　王　平
譯　書　薛慧儀
發行人　劉振強
著作財　三民書局股份有限公司
產權人　臺北市復興北路386號
發行所　三民書局股份有限公司
　　　　地址／臺北市復興北路386號
　　　　電話／(02)25006600
　　　　郵撥／0009998-5
印刷所　三民書局股份有限公司
門市部　復北店／臺北市復興北路386號
　　　　重南店／臺北市重慶南路一段61號
初版一刷　2003年7月
編　號　S 85645-1
定　價　新臺幣壹佰捌拾元整
行政院新聞局登記證局版臺業字第○二○○號

ISBN　957-14-3767-0　（精裝）